MARCELLA'S HOUSE

PLAYHOUSE

TOOL SHED

PLAYROOM

This book belongs to:

_____

Raggedy Ann & Andy's

GROW AND LEARN LIBRARY

VOLUME 15

RAGGEDY ANDY'S PERFECT PARTY

A LYNX BOOK

This book is published by Lynx Books, a division of Lynx Communications, Inc., 41 Madison Avenue, New York, New York 10010. The name "Lynx" together with the logotype consisting of a stylized head of a lynx is a trademark of Lynx Communications, Inc.

Raggedy Ann and Andy's Grow-and-Learn Library, the names and depictions of Raggedy Ann, Raggedy Andy and all related characters are trademarks of Macmillan, Inc.

Raggedy Andy looked at the calendar on the playroom wall.

"Hooray!" he shouted. "Today is the first day of summer! We'll have lots and lots of sunny days to play ball and go on picnics! Summers are so much fun!"

Raggedy Dog came to see what was going on. "Why are you so happy?" he asked.

"Today is the first day of summer," Raggedy Andy told him. "We should have a big celebration! With a parade! And marching bands! And floats! And batons twirling in the air! And . . ."

"Wouldn't that be a lot for us to do in just one day?" asked Raggedy Ann.

"I guess it *is* too much," said Raggedy Andy. "But we ought to do something to celebrate. I know. I'll give a party instead."

"Great!" barked Raggedy Dog. He wagged his tail with delight.

"First," said Raggedy Andy, "I'll make a list of all the things that need to be done. That's the best way to start."

He found a big, fat pencil and a clean sheet of paper.

"Let's see," he said. "We'll have the party outside in the backyard. Now, what do we need to make this the best party ever?"

"Guests!" said Raggedy Ann. "Who's going to come to the party?" she asked.

"Everyone!" said Raggedy Andy. "I want to invite all the dolls and toys in the playroom. After all, it's the first day of summer for them, too."

"Hooray!" barked Raggedy Dog, who trotted away happily to tell the others.

Raggedy Andy thought aloud. "We need a big table and chairs and plates and cups and games and decorations and . . ."

Scritch, scritch, scritch, went his pencil. As he wrote, the list became longer and longer and longer!

"What a lot of work!" Raggedy Andy said, rubbing his head. "How will I ever get all this done?"

Just then Raggedy Dog came running back. Right behind him was Babette the French Doll. And behind her was Percy the Policeman Doll. And behind him was Tim the Toy Soldier. Then Sunny Bunny. And Bubbles the Clown Doll.

"We'll help!" Babette said.

"We want to celebrate the first day of summer, too," said Percy.

"We want to help to make this a perfect party," Sunny Bunny added.

Raggedy Andy spread the long list out on the floor, and all the dolls crowded around him. Each of them picked something to do.

All morning long the dolls worked to get ready for Raggedy Andy's party.

Percy the Policeman and Tim the Toy Soldier set up a table in the backyard.

"There!" Percy grunted as he pushed the last little bench into place. "There's a place for everyone to sit."

Raggedy Andy happily crossed "table" and "chairs" off his list.

Bubbles the Clown staggered outside with a big pile of cups and saucers from the tea party set. Then he ran back for the little plates and forks.

Next came Babette, carrying a pile of pink napkins decorated with pictures of buttercups and daisies. Babette placed one napkin beside each plate.

Raggedy Andy was so pleased with the way things were going that he quite forgot that no one had volunteered to hang the party decorations.

Raggedy Ann smiled at her brother as she brought out a beautiful cake all covered with flowers and little birds. Raggedy Ann had made the cake in Marcella's play oven.

Greta the Dutch Doll brought over an apronful of
berries that she had picked in the garden.
Raggedy Dog and Raggedy Cat brought flowers for
the table.

"Cups! Plates! Cake! Flowers!" Raggedy Andy noticed that his list was becoming shorter and shorter.

"Hey, Raggedy Andy, who's going to hang the decorations?" called Tallyho the Wooden Horse, as he helped Raggedy Ann set up the "Pin the Petals on the Daisy" game.

"Whoooah!" shouted Raggedy Andy, suddenly seeing the last word on his list: DECORATIONS. If he didn't get those decorations up in a hurry, his perfect party would be ruined!

"I know," he thought. "I'll do them myself. No problem. All I need is a ladder."

He looked inside the toolshed for a nice, sturdy ladder.
He saw a wheelbarrow. And a watering can . . .

But no ladder.

   He searched inside the playhouse. There were books
and boxes to stand on . . .

But no ladder!
    Raggedy Andy went back outside and looked up at the lowest branches of the trees.

"I'll never be able to hang anything way up there without a ladder," he moaned.

What would he do with the fat, bouncy balloons that Sunny Bunny and Babette were blowing up?

"You could stand on my back," suggested The Camel with the Wrinkled Knees.

"Not high enough," said Raggedy Andy.

"Maybe I could flip you up in the air," said Bubbles the Clown.

"I don't think so," said Raggedy Andy, shaking his yarn hair.

"Is there anything I can do to help?" rumbled a deep, sleepy voice.

All the dolls and toys stopped talking and looked across the yard. Daphne the Dinosaur Doll strolled out from the garden.

"Hello, Daphne, where have you been?" asked Raggedy Andy with surprise.

"I was taking a nap behind the tall grass. All this noise woke me up, so I came to see what was going on," said Daphne.

"Raggedy Andy is giving a party to celebrate the first day of summer," Raggedy Ann told her. "We all pitched in to help him."

"But I can't find a way to hang the decorations. And we really want everything to be perfect," Raggedy Andy added.

"*Hmmm. . .*" Daphne began. Then she smiled. She leaned over and whispered into Raggedy Andy's ear. "What do you think of . . . *buzz, buzz, buzz?*"

"What a great idea!" he cried.

"Then let's go," said Daphne.

Daphne knelt down next to a bunch of streamers and
balloons. Raggedy Andy picked them up and stepped lightly
onto the bottom of her tail. Then, one by one, he climbed
up the ridges on her back.

He climbed right up until he reached the tippity top of Daphne's neck. Raggedy Andy pinned the streamers to the outside of the playhouse. Then he hung the balloons from the branches of the trees.

As he came down, everyone clapped.

"There," said Raggedy Ann. "Thanks to you, Raggedy Andy, we're going to have a wonderful party."
Raggedy Andy smiled and looked around at his friends.

"Not just thanks to me," he said. "Let's face it. We all did hard jobs. But it took all of us working together to make this a really perfect party. Happy first day of summer!"